J
FICTION   Auch, Mary Jane.
AUCH   I was a third grade
           bodyguard.

DATE			

I Was A Third Grade Bodyguard

I Was A Third Grade Bodyguard

by Mary Jane Auch
illustrated by Herm Auch

Holiday House / New York

Library of Congress Cataloging-in-Publication Data

Auch, Mary Jane.
I was a third grade bodyguard / by Mary Jane Auch;
illustrated by Herm Auch.—1st ed.
p. cm.
Summary: When Brian takes care of the third-grade
class's pet chicken during Christmas vacation,
Arful, his talking dog, has his paws full watching over it.
ISBN 0-8234-1775-1
[1. Dogs—Fiction. 2. Chickens—Fiction. 3. Pets—Fiction.
4. Christmas—Fiction.] I. Auch, Herm, ill. II. Title.
PZ7.A898 Iac 2003
[Fic]—dc21   2002068869

To Patience Brewster
and Bruce Coville,
who helped with many of the imaginative
names Tallulah calls Arful.

Chapter One

My name is Arful and I'm a dog. I can also talk—not woofy dog talk, but peoplespeak. It happened because of something that went wrong in a science project, but that's a whole other story. Right now I'm waiting for Brian—he's my human—and his friends Josh and Dougie to come from school. And today is even better than a regular day because it's the beginning of Christmas vacation. Brian will be home for a whole week.

Here come Josh and Dougie now, but Brian isn't with them. Dougie runs right over to scratch me behind the ears. He's the world's best ear scratcher. And he doesn't change his clothes too often, so he smells really great.

"Hey, Arful," Dougie says. "Wait till you see the surprise Brian has for you."

Right away I'm thinking food. Brian is heading for me now, carrying something wrapped in a blanket. *BowWOW!* It must be a really big snack.

"Arful," Brian says. "I have a special treat for you. Meet Tallulah, our class chicken."

A beady-eyed head with a sharp beak peeks out over the blanket. My favorite dog food is made of chicken. I'm getting a whole chicken all to myself? This is the best surprise ever!

"Bri-an! Wait up!" It's that nasty Emily Venable. She and her two friends, Lissa and Cara, are running our way. The boys don't like them, so we keep going, but the girls catch up anyway.

Emily walks backward in front of Brian so he can't get around her. "You know I wanted to take Tallulah home over vacation. I can't believe Mrs. Metz picked you instead of me. I had my doll four-poster all made up for her. I even made her some little sheets with a chicken print on them."

Dougie laughs. "Chickens sleeping in beds? That's how much you know about chickens." Dougie knows a lot about chickens because he and his grandmother have a whole flock of them on their farm. Part of the reason Dougie smells so good is that he has to collect

the eggs before school and he always has chicken manure on his shoes.

"Oh, yeah?" Lissa says. "I bet Brian hasn't even thought about where she'll sleep at his house. Have you, Brian?"

Emily is looking at me. "That's not the worst of it. Brian's house isn't even safe. Brian's dog could eat her."

Well, duh! That's my plan. My mouth waters just thinking about it.

Emily points at me. "See? He's drooling already!"

Cara comes over to pet me. She's the nice one. "Aw, Arful is a sweetie. He wouldn't hurt a flea, would you, Arful?"

I want to tell her I probably hurt my fleas when I scratch and bite at them, but I'm not allowed to talk to anybody but Brian, Dougie, and Josh.

Brian and Emily are still arguing about the chicken. "What Tallulah does at my house is my business," Brian says. "So just keep your nose out of it."

"What happens to Tallulah is everybody's business in our whole class," Emily calls out as we walk away. "I'll be watching you, Brian Lewis!"

I can hardly wait to get home. Chicken dinner, here I come! I try to peek under the blanket my meal is wrapped in.

The chicken's head jerks around to look at me. "What are you staring at?" she asks. She's talking in chickenspeak. I can understand her, but to Brian, Josh, and Dougie, she's just clucking. "Don't even think about it, bucko!" she says.

A snack with an attitude. Hoooo boy! This is going to be fun! I do love a challenge.

Chapter Two

We're in Brian's room now. Must be almost time for my treat. "Arful, make sure Tallulah stays in my room," Brian says. "Mom doesn't know about me bringing her home yet. I'm going downstairs for a glass of milk." He closes the door behind him.

Milk with chicken? Why not? Milk with cookies is good.

Tallulah is sitting in the middle of the bed, watching me. "Don't try anything funny, bonehead," she says.

"I don't know what you're talking about," I say in dogspeak, sidling over to the bed. Even though we all sound different, most animals can understand each other. It's sort of like humans who speak the same language with different accents. I rest my chin on the comforter. "I only want to make you feel at home." I'm trying real hard to sound convincing and trying even harder not to drool. I've never tasted fresh chicken before.

Tallulah keeps blinking and jerking her head around. Sheesh! She's a nervous wreck. "Want to watch TV?" I ask, trying to calm her down. "Brian gets the animal channel."

"If you think I'm going to watch a bunch of dumb dogs running around an obstacle course, you're crazy," Tallulah says. "What they need is a chicken channel. Now, that would be worth watching." She has a heavy chicken accent, but I can understand her.

"Maybe they do have a chicken channel," I say. I pick up the remote in my mouth, put it on Brian's desk, line it up with the TV, and start punching the buttons with my nose.

"That big snout of yours hits four channels at once," Tallulah says. "Let me do it." She comes over and pecks at the buttons with her beak. "There, that's better. A show about flying reindeer. We animals who can fly are superior to you poor fools who have to run around on the ground, you know."

"Maybe I can't fly, but I can talk," I say.

"Big deal! You think you're the first dog I ever talked to?"

"I mean I can talk peoplespeak."

"Yeah, right." Tallulah laughs. Chicken laughter is a nasty sound.

"I'll prove it to you when Brian comes back."

"Whatever." Tallulah turns around a few times on the pillow to make herself a little nest. "Just be quiet so I can watch my show."

I ease over to the head of the bed. She's busy watching the TV now, so she's not paying any attention to me. If I just get a little closer, I can reach over and . . .

"Arful! Let go of that chicken!" Brian is standing in the doorway with a look of panic on his face.

I let go and Tallulah pecks me on the nose. "Ow!"

"Serves you right." Brian grabs Tallulah and holds her out of my reach. She flaps her wings and gets away from him.

"But I thought you brought her home as a treat for me."

"Not that kind of a treat! I thought you two could be friends. Besides, bringing her home over vacation is a real honor." Brian's voice is muffled because he's crawling under the bed, trying to find Tallulah. When he finally drags her out, they're both covered with dust bunnies.

Tallulah is glaring at me. "If you ever try anything like that again, dribble lips, I'll peck your nose clean off."

My stomach is churning, so I let out a little puff of gas, which calms me down a little. I think of it as "aroma" therapy.

Tallulah starts fanning the air with her wing. "Hey, gas bag, knock off the air pollution!"

"She's calling me names," I tell Brian.

Brian is busy picking the dust bunnies off Tallulah's comb. "Listen, Arful. Tallulah has lived in the school for four years. Our class hatched her for Easter when we were in kindergarten. Every year she moves up a grade with us. This is the very first time I've been allowed to bring her home. If anything happens to her over vacation, nobody will ever speak to me again."

"But she's only a chicken!"

"You are the dumbest, ugliest dog I've ever seen," Tallulah says.

"If it weren't for Brian, I'd swallow you whole," I say in dogspeak.

Brian beams at us. "Now, that's better. You two are getting to be friends already."

Chapter Three

Brian goes on and on about how Tallulah is the class mascot and how important she is. If he just said I couldn't eat her, I could go along with that. But then he says I have to like her, which is impossible because she's nasty.

Then he says the worst thing of all. "Think of yourself as Tallulah's bodyguard, Arful. You can't let anything happen to her, no matter what." All of a sudden I'm the bodyguard for a chicken with a rotten personality! "Do you understand, Arful?"

"Yes," I mumble in peoplespeak. The only good thing is that Tallulah can't understand what Brian is saying. At least she'll still be afraid of me and stay out of my way.

The only reason I understand peoplespeak is because of this science fair project when Brian tried to hypnotize me. A whole bunch of things went wrong, and I ended up talking like a kid. I even understand what I'm saying—at least I think I do.

"Now, this is a test, Arful," Brian says. "I'm going downstairs to call Josh and Dougie. When I get back, I don't want to see one ruffled feather on that chicken's body. Do you understand?"

I sigh. "Yes."

"Promise?"

"I promise."

The door barely closes behind Brian, when Tallulah sashays across the floor. "Now, this is a test, Arful," she clucks in a singsongy chickenspeak voice. Did she understand what Brian just said? Must be a coincidence.

I lie down in the farthest corner of the room, but I'm keeping my eye on her. She stretches out her wings and twirls around in the middle of the floor like a model. "See these feathers all over my body? Not one of them better be ruffled when Brian gets back."

I put my head on my paws and pretend to be asleep, but I can hear the *click-skritch* of chicken feet coming across the bare floor. Then I feel chicken breath on my nose. "Wake up, liver lips! You're supposed to be guarding me."

"I don't know what you're talking about." I cover my ears with my paws.

She gives me a peck on the head. "Brian said you have to protect me."

"You understand peoplespeak?"

"Why wouldn't I? I've been in school since I hatched. I'm a whiz at math, too. I can multiply in my head. Ask me a math question."

"Leave me alone."

"Aw, come on. Ask me a hard one. How about 467 times 895?"

"Go away!"

"It's 417,965. Ask me another one."

"No!"

"Okay, you don't like math. How about geography? What's the capital of Turkmenistan?"

I can't believe this. It was bad enough when Tallulah was just obnoxious, but now she's some sort of a chicken genius. Brian's real smart, too. If he finds out about Tallulah, he might like her better than me. But wait! Brian can't understand what she's saying, unless . . . "Hey, Tallulah. If you're so smart, can you talk peoplespeak?"

She doesn't say anything, just blinks and jerks her head around.

"Well, can you?"

Her head is jerking around so fast, she looks like one of those bobbley things people put in the back windows of their cars.

"Aha!" I say. "I guess you're not so smart after all."

"I'm smart enough to outwit you anytime I want to, droopy ears. Did you know that most of a dog's brain is devoted to the sense of smell?"

"Yeah, right."

"It's true, nose brain. I can show you a diagram in Brian's science book." She flies up to Brian's desk and flips through the book until she gets to a picture that's supposed to be a dog brain. Most of it is labeled "smell."

Tallulah is standing there with her wings on her hips—at least I think they're her hips. "That doesn't leave many brain cells for important stuff, does it? Hmmmmmm?"

I don't answer her. I had no idea that they were teaching Brian anti-dog propaganda in school. That's terrible. Who knows what they've been saying about me?

I don't have any time to worry about this, though, because suddenly there's a scream, and my first test as a chicken bodyguard starts with something crashing down about two inches from Tallulah's head.

Chapter Four

Everything is a blur. The crashing thing hits again, bouncing off Tallulah's back. She takes off and lands on top of Brian's bookcase.

There's another scream. I turn to see Brian's mother going after Tallulah with a broom. At first this makes me happy. Then I remember that if anything happens to that chicken, I'm in big trouble.

"Stop!" I yell in peoplespeak just as Mrs. Lewis swings again. "Don't hit her! She's the class chicken!"

The broom misses Tallulah's head but knocks her off the bookcase. Tallulah lands on the floor, dazed. I grab her by the neck and make a dash for the door. Mrs. Lewis screams and gets out of the way, but I

run smack into Brian coming up the stairs. I let go of Tallulah, and she flaps over the stair railing and down to the front hall.

"Arful, what are you doing? I couldn't trust you for two minutes?"

A chicken feather floats down from somewhere above us and lands on my nose. Mrs. Lewis is staring at me. "Brian, where were you just now?"

"Down in the kitchen. I only left my room for a minute. And Arful promised not to hurt the chicken."

"He promised?" Mrs. Lewis asks, leaning in closer. "How did he promise?"

"I mean, I thought I had Arful trained to leave the chicken alone. And I can explain why I had a chicken in my room."

"Never mind that," Mrs. Lewis says. "Just now someone yelled at me not to hurt the chicken. I know this sounds crazy, but I think . . . well, I think it was Arful."

Brian gives me a look. I broke the no-peoplespeak rule. Brian doesn't want anybody except Josh and Dougie to know I can talk. He's afraid if other people find out, it will make me famous and they'll take me off to someplace called holly wood. I don't know where that is, but I know there's a holly bush in Brian's back-yard and the leaves have little prickly things all over them. So I'm not keen on going to this prickly holly wood place.

Brian pretends to laugh. "That's really funny, Mom. A talking dog."

"I know what I heard, Brian. Listen to this." Mrs. Lewis moves close to me. "Arful, speak."

Brian looks panicked when I open my mouth, but I just make those woofy sounds dogs make when their people tell them to speak. Any dog can do that, and we only do it to humor our people because we're not speaking any real dog words. And when people think we're just making little growls and squeals, that's when we're really passing on some important information to other dogs.

Brian gives me a thumbs-up sign behind his mother's back. "It was probably your conscience talking, Mom. You belong to all those groups about not hurting animals and all."

Mrs. Lewis puts her arm around Brian. "That makes sense. Of course I wasn't thinking about the fact that I was hurting an animal. I just opened the door to clean your room and there was this . . . this thing. I just started lashing out. Oh, I'm so ashamed of myself." Mrs. Lewis bites on her knuckle.

Brian pats his mother on the shoulder. "It's okay, Mom. I was coming downstairs to tell you that we have the honor of keeping Tallulah over Christmas vacation. I knew you would be pleased on account of you loving animals so much."

"Oh, I am pleased, dear. I'm thrilled. I'm going to find that chicken and make it up to her right now. I just got some fresh bean sprouts from the health food store."

Brian closes the door as soon as she leaves. "What is the matter with you? I told you to guard Tallulah, then I find her in your mouth again."

"But I was rescuing her! Your mother tried to bash Tallulah in the head with a broom."

"You talked, Arful. I can't believe you talked in front of my mother."

"Well, it's a good thing I did. If I hadn't yelled for her to stop, that chicken would be nuggets by now."

Brian shakes his head. "I just don't know if I can trust you anymore. You may be able to talk, but sometimes I wonder how much you understand inside that dog brain of yours."

It hurts my feelings to hear Brian say things like that. Maybe Tallulah is right. Maybe the school teaches kids that dogs are dumb. I bet that science book was written by somebody who never met a dog. Probably somebody who loves chickens.

Nobody ever said a chicken is a man's best friend.

Chapter Five

Saturday morning Brian says he's taking Tallulah and me over to Dougie's house. Mrs. Lewis stops decorating the Christmas tree and makes a big fuss about him taking the chicken out in the cold.

I go over to sniff the tree. Another dog has put his mark on one of the lower branches. It happened when Dr. Lewis left this tree leaning against the garage for a whole day before he brought it in. None of the humans in the house even noticed. You'd think the little yellow icicles hanging off the branch would have been a dead giveaway. Now the icicles have melted, but the scent hits me in the face every time I come into the house. I really want to put my own mark over it. I don't, though, because I know

I'm not supposed to lift my leg on anything in the house.

Brian and his mother are still arguing about taking Tallulah outside. Mrs. Lewis pulls some boxes off a shelf in the hall closet. "Here, this should keep her warm. It's one of your baby sweaters."

"It's pink!" Brian says.

"Well, I was planning on a girl," Mrs. Lewis says, then notices the expression on Brian's face. "Not that I was ever disappointed that you were a boy. No sirree. Not for one single second."

"You made me wear a pink sweater?" He looks in the box. "All of this stuff is pink!"

"Well, after this fortune-teller told me I was having a girl, I found all these adorable pink baby clothes on sale. And then, of course, I couldn't return them."

"You had me dressed in pink all the time? Isn't that child abuse?" Mrs. Lewis isn't listening. She keeps pulling out little pink sweaters and holding them up to Tallulah. I notice she isn't worried about *me* being out in the cold without a sweater.

"Aw, Mom. Tallulah doesn't need clothes. She has feathers."

Mrs. Lewis gives Brian a look. "Would you go out in weather like this wearing nothing but feathers?"

"I don't see the birds on your feeder wearing little sweaters."

"That's because they don't have anyone to worry about them." She's trying to get one of Tallulah's wings into a sleeve but finally gives up and just buttons up the front. She pulls out a little baby cap with pink roses on it, but it's about four times too big. Chickens have really small heads. Can't be much of

a brain inside there. Why didn't I think of that when Tallulah was making nasty remarks about a dog's brain?

Mrs. Lewis gives up on the baby bonnets and pulls one of the sleeves of the sweater over Tallulah's head so the cuff makes a little cap.

I can't help laughing. Dog laughter can't be heard by humans, but Tallulah whips her head around to glare at me. The cuff slips down over her eyes. "Don't start with me, wag rump," she says.

"I can't wait until Dougie's chickens get a load of you," I say. Dougie's chickens are tough. They wouldn't be caught dead wearing pink sweaters. He has a rooster, too. Dougie calls him Herman the Terminator because he's always in a bad mood and nobody messes with him. This is going to be fun.

Dougie's farm is just beyond the edge of town, so it's a pretty long walk. As we pass the last house, I catch sight of the Christmas tree on top of their silo. I can smell the chickens now. I don't know why nobody ever thought of bottling the smell of chicken manure. It's beautiful. Sure would sell better than that perfume stuff.

Josh is already at Dougie's house when we arrive. He's helping Dougie build a snow horse. I jump up on Josh and lick his cheek. He likes that.

Dougie is the first one to notice Tallulah. "What's the hen dressed up for?"

"Mom thought she might get cold."

"That's the goofiest-looking thing I ever saw." He comes closer to get a better look. "What is this thing? A baby sweater?"

Brian shrugs. "It's something Mom had in the closet."

Now Josh is getting in on the act. "One of your old baby sweaters, Brian? A *pink* baby sweater?"

Dougie laughs and smacks Brian on the back so hard, he almost knocks the breath out of him. "Little Brian wore a pretty pink sweater?"

"It was white," Brian says, choking. "Mom washed it with a pair of red socks and they ran."

Dougie is doing a little dance around Brian. "Aw, you sure your name isn't Brianna?"

The sleeve has slid down to cover Tallulah's whole head now. She looks like a sock puppet.

"Leave him alone, Dougie," Josh says. "Washing a white sweater with red socks is exactly the flaky kind of thing Brian's mother would do."

"Yeah, I know," Dougie says. "But it was funny picturing baby Brian in a pink sweater."

Brian pulls the sleeve off Tallulah's head. "We're wasting time. Let's start the experiment."

"What experiment?" Dougie asks.

"Brian wants to see if a chicken raised in a school can get along with chickens raised in a barn," Josh says. "He's going to write up the results for extra credit in science."

Dougie shakes his head. "You and your experiments. I can tell you one thing right now. If you don't take that sweater off her, my grandma's chickens will laugh your chicken right out of the barn."

As we head toward the barn, Brian is fumbling in his pocket. "Wait a minute. I must have lost my pencil on the way over. I have to go back home and get another one."

"You think I live in a cave?" Dougie says. "I have pencils."

"Pencils you haven't chewed on?" Brian asks. "I can't write with a chewed pencil."

"Jeez, Brian," Josh says. "If it has lead, what difference does it make if there are a few chew marks?"

"That's right," I say. "I like sticks with chew marks. They're more interesting. Especially if another dog was doing the chewing, because then I can look at the teeth marks and try to figure out what kind of dog it was, and sometimes if I sniff it, I can tell what he just ate, and if I . . ."

"Cut it out!" Brian yells. "I want a pencil without chew marks! Is that too much to ask?"

Dougie shrugs. "All right. Come on in and look for yourself." We all follow him, but he stops us at the door. "Grandma won't let that chicken into the house even if she is wearing your pretty pink baby sweater."

Brian turns and shoves Tallulah into Josh's arms.

"Hey," Josh says. "I'm not staying out here with the chicken."

"We'll be right back." Brian closes the door.

"I smell cookies," I say.

Josh sniffs. "You sure?"

I don't know why humans bother to have a nose at all. The air on this porch is screaming cookies, and Josh has to ask? "Yup, it's cookies, all right. Christmas cookies. Wait a minute." I take a long, slow sniff. "They have sugar sprinkles on top. . . ." Another sniff. This time I flare out my nostrils. "The sprinkles are red. And the cookies are in the shape of stars."

Josh's eyes are bugging out of his head. "You can tell what color sprinkles and what shape they are just by smelling?"

"I was only kidding about the shape, but I know the

smell of red sprinkles. You have no idea what a wonderful machine a dog's nose is. I smell milk, too."

Josh peeks in the kitchen window. "You're right. They're sitting at the table having milk and cookies with red sprinkles. Hey, they *are* star-shaped. Arful, you're a genius!"

"Just ask him a math question," Tallulah clucks. "You'll see how much of a genius he is."

Josh sets Tallulah down next to me. "I gotta get in there. Arful, you watch Tallulah."

"Wait! I can't! She'll run away."

"Yeah, you're right." He looks around, then dumps some rotten potatoes out of a bushel basket that's sitting on the porch steps. He puts the basket upside down over Tallulah like a cage. "She's not going anywhere now. Just watch her."

"I love cookies, too!" I say, but Josh goes inside without answering me and I'm left with Tallulah. I can see her beady little eyes watching me through the basket slats.

Chapter Six

"Hey, warden," Tallulah says.

I don't answer her.

"You with the big, fancy nose. If you spring me out of here, I'll get you one of those cookies."

Now she has my interest. "How can you do that?"

"Easy. I saw a partly open window around the back of the house. I can squeeze through, sneak into the kitchen, and grab a cookie."

"They'll see you."

"No, they won't, because you're going to bark when I get into the room. When they all look over here to see what's going on, I'll swoop in on the table and be out of there before they turn around."

"I don't know. It sounds risky."

"It's up to you. I'm not the one who wanted a Christmas cookie with red sprinkles. Mmmmmm. They sure smell good, don't they? I can just imagine how those sugar sprinkles melt in your mouth. But I'm sure that's no big deal for you. You probably get them every day, right?"

I think about Mrs. Lewis's cookies. I don't know which ones are worse—the soybean cookies shaped like Christmas trees with chopped spinach sprinkled on top to make them green, or the rutabaga cookies shaped like Santa Clauses with little red pimiento hats. Just thinking about Mrs. Lewis's Christmas cookies makes me shiver. I'm usually not fussy about what I eat, but those things are nasty.

I decide it's worth the risk. I lift the basket. "All right. Go for it." Tallulah takes off running toward the back of the house. I look into the kitchen. The boys are stuffing cookies into their mouths. Tallulah had better hurry up or there won't be any left. I watch the door that goes from the kitchen to the living room. That must be where Tallulah will come through. They're down to two cookies! Where is she?

All of a sudden I hear cackling behind me. I look over my shoulder and see Tallulah running toward the barn. She tricked me!

"Hey!" I bark, bounding off the porch. "Hey hey hey, *HEY*!"

Tallulah runs through the barn door. I can hear a burst of chicken laughter. By the time I get inside, a big red hen is circling Tallulah, giving her a good looking-over. "What's this, a fashion show? You one of those supermodel chickens?"

"She's no model," clucks a speckled hen. "She's too scrawny. They like the big, plump chickens to model in the chicken commercials."

These hens know a lot about commercials. Dougie's grandmother has an old TV going in the barn in the wintertime. She says it keeps her hens laying when everybody else's birds quit for the winter. Brian thinks it has something to do with the kind of rays that the TV gives out. He's doing research on that, too. Dougie thinks they just like the soap operas.

An old gray hen pulls at Tallulah's sleeve. "Whaddya call this contraption?"

Tallulah whips her head around. "If you know what's good for you, you won't mess with me."

"Oh, yeah? Who says?" A scruffy-looking white hen is coming at Tallulah now. I skid to a stop next to Tallulah and look around the barn. *All* of the hens are coming at us.

"I says, that's who." Tallulah tries to flap her wings, but she can't because of the sweater. All she's able to do is swing her sleeves a little, which doesn't scare anybody.

"Shhh!" I whisper in her ear, or at least where I think her ear must be.

"Don't shush me," she squawks. "You think I'm afraid of these stupid barn hens?"

If all of these hens decide to attack Tallulah at once, I don't stand a chance of fighting them off. Just thinking about all those sharp beaks makes my nose hurt. They always go for the nose.

"Pleeeeeeze be quiet," I whisper.

"Who you calling stupid?" Big Red is almost in Tallulah's face now.

"All right, calm down," I say. "Tallulah didn't mean anything. Just back off, all of you."

Big Red turns to me. I notice she's very tall for a chicken. Also very wide. In a dark room she could pass for a turkey. "You back off, bubba," she says.

"Okay, okay. I'm backing, see? And Tallulah's backing, too. We're just backing right out of here. Everybody have a nice day."

Tallulah is not backing. She is beak to beak with Big Red. Before I can stop her, they're fighting in a blur of red feathers and pink sleeves.

Brian yells from the door. "Arful! Don't let Tallulah get hurt."

"She started it!"

"I don't care who started it. Help her!"

By now every hen in the place wants a piece of Tallulah. I take a deep breath and run right into the middle of the fight. "All right, ladies! Ow! Everybody, just calm down. Ow, ow! Ladies, please! Ow, ow, AOOOOOOOW!"

"Awesome fight!" Dougie yells. "You go, Arful!"

I would love to go, but I can't go anywhere. I have a hen on my head and at least two on my back. Everyone has forgotten about Tallulah. Now they all want a piece of me. The only thing I can do is crouch and cover my nose with my paws.

Then, just when I think things can't get much worse, things get much worse.

A big voice booms out over the squawking. "Leave my hens alone!" I don't have to look up to know who it is. It's Herman the Terminator.

Herman is a bulldozer with feathers. He plows right over me, flattening me into the straw on the floor. When I finally struggle to my feet, Herman and Tallulah are nowhere in sight.

"They got outside!" Brian yells. We all run outdoors and look around. "There aren't any tracks," I say.

"Of course not," Brian says. "You don't leave tracks when you're flying." He thinks I'm stupid. I know he does. I can tell by the look on his face. He's never looked at me like that before.

But then Dougie takes my side. "Arful is right, Brian. Chickens can't fly that far. Especially Tallulah. She's never had any practice. So there would be tracks where she landed. Maybe she and Herman are still in the barn."

"I know they got out," Brian says. "I felt the breeze as they flew past me. Come on, help me look. They must be close by."

We look in all the little shacks and buildings around the farm. I try to tell them that Tallulah's scent isn't here, but nobody pays any attention to me, not even Dougie. Finally Brian says we should give up and go home.

Chapter Seven

We're back at Brian's house and everybody is mad at me. But I'm not the only one in trouble.

"Why didn't you hang on to Tallulah, Josh?" Brian yells.

"But Arful said he'd watch her."

"Arful says a lot of things. Half the time he doesn't even know what he's talking about. He's a dog, Josh."

Josh shrugs his shoulders. "I didn't think Arful would have to do anything. I thought the basket was heavy enough to hold her. Besides, you guys were sitting in there having cookies."

"We were going to bring some out to you," Brian says.

Dougie grins. "Yeah, right."

"We have to do something." Brian sounds like he's ready to cry. "Tallulah will freeze to death out there."

"Well, at least she's wearing a sweater," Josh says.

Brian smacks him in the arm. "A lot you care."

"I do care. Look, how about we make posters and put them up around town? We can have all of our phone numbers on the posters so anyone who finds her can call us."

"But I don't want anyone to know she's lost," Brian says. "Emily will ruin me if she finds out."

"You'd better find Tallulah fast," Dougie says. "Chickens don't take to the cold, you know."

Brian sighs. "All right. I guess we don't have a choice." He gets out paper and crayons and they all start drawing.

"Should we draw her with the pink sweater?" Dougie asks.

Brian shakes his head. "She might have lost it by now. Besides, how many chickens will be walking down the street this time of year? We probably don't even need a picture." He looks over at Dougie's poster. "Wanted, dead or alive!" He smacks Dougie in the arm. I dive under the table. I've never seen Brian this mad before.

Brian grabs Dougie's poster and rips it up. "Everything is a joke to you. Just go home. Josh and I will do the posters."

Dougie gets up and puts on his jacket. "Fine. I'm out of here."

He hasn't been gone more than a couple of minutes, when the doorbell rings.

"It's Dougie coming back to apologize," Brian says.

I go over and sniff at the crack under the door. "It's not Dougie. I can't quite place the scent, but I know it's somebody I don't like. Don't open the door."

Brian ignores me and goes to open it anyway. It's the girls. Emily pushes right past Brian and comes into the room.

Brian's mouth drops open. "What . . . what are you doing here?"

"I told you I'd be watching you, Brian," Emily says. "We came over to make sure you're taking good care of Tallulah."

I can smell Brian start to sweat. Maybe next time I warn him about something, he'll listen to me.

"Guests are supposed to be invited," Josh says. "I don't remember inviting you."

"Of course you didn't invite us, because you don't

live here, do you, Josh?" Emily shoves him aside and comes into the room. The other girls follow her.

Brian turns the posters over. "Well, I live here and I didn't invite you, either."

"Oh, really? My mistake." Emily gives him that weird little smile she has. She may be smiling, but she's not being nice. A dog can tell.

Cara and Lissa are looking all over the living room, making little *buk-buk-buk* hen noises. Funny, I never heard humans do that before. I wonder if they know they're saying, "I'm laying an egg any second now."

"We didn't come to see you two," Emily says. "We came to visit Tallulah."

"She's sleeping," Brian says.

Emily holds out a little silver bag. "Go wake her up. I brought a Christmas present for her."

"You're early," Josh says. "Christmas isn't for two more days."

Cara is on her hands and knees, telling the dust bunnies under the couch about the egg she's laying.

"So, Tallulah will open her present early." Emily heads for the stairs. "Is she up in your room? I want to see if she likes her present."

Brian blocks her way. "No! I mean yes, she's in my room, but no, I can't wake her up. My mother says Tallulah needs to get more sleep. She's too nervous."

Lissa laughs. "That's silly. Chickens always act nervous."

"My mother knows about these things," Brian says. "She's practically a chicken expert."

Emily looks all mean and squinty-eyed now. She sticks her finger in Brian's chest. "You're lying, Brian Lewis. There's a reason you don't want us to see Tallulah. I think something has happened to her. She's hurt, isn't she?"

"No, she's fine. Just sleeping is all." Brian tries to back away from Emily, but she keeps after him, jabbing that finger.

"She's hurt or sick or . . ." Emily's eyes get wide. "Your dog ate her, didn't he? Your ugly dog ate our class chicken."

"I wish!" I say in dogspeak.

Emily is sticking her finger in Brian's face now. "Tallulah is dead, isn't she, huh? Admit it, Brian."

"No!"

"Okay, if she's not dead, bring her out so we can see her."

Uh-oh! This is not good. This is not good at all. I have to help. Maybe I should bite somebody. No, wait, biting is bad. Barking is better. "Bark!" I yell.

"Barkity-bark-bark!" I jump up on Emily and push her toward the front door.

"Get your dog away from me!"

Now I go after Lissa and slobber all over her. "Barkity-bark!" Dripity-drip.

"Eeeeeeew! Dog drool!" She trips all over herself trying to get to the front door.

I don't do anything to Cara. I like her and I know she likes me. But she follows her friends out of the house.

"I'll get to the bottom of this, Brian Lewis," Emily yells over her shoulder. "I'm coming back tomorrow to find out what you did to Tallulah. And if anything has happened to that chicken, I'm going to tell our teacher, and the principal, and every kid in our class! I'll even call the newspaper and TV station!"

Josh slams the door after them. Brian plops down on the couch and covers his eyes with his hands. "When we go back to school, everybody is going to hate me."

Josh sits next to him. "Don't worry, Brian. Emily's only bluffing. She doesn't know what happened."

Brian looks up. "Well, neither do we! For all we know, Tallulah's either frozen to death, run over by a car, or eaten by some animal."

"Now, that really makes me mad," I say. "You told me I couldn't eat Tallulah, and I didn't. But if some other animal gets to eat her, well, that's just not fair. Not fair at all."

Brian is staring at me.

"What?" I ask. *"What?"*

"All you ever think about is eating!" Brian yells. "If you hadn't let Tallulah go, we wouldn't be in this mess. You may talk like a person, but you still think like a dog. Because of you, I'm not going to have a single friend after this."

I want to tell Brian I'll still be his friend no matter what happens. But Brian doesn't want me for a friend anymore. Maybe he will if I can find Tallulah. That's my only hope. I can feel my tail drooping between my legs as I creep quietly into the kitchen and out my doggie door.

But I will love Brian even if he hates me forever. What can I say? I'm a dog. A dog is your friend for life.

Chapter Eight

It's snowing again. That's bad. It's hard to catch a scent when tracks are covered by snow. I'm going to Dougie's house because that's where I saw Tallulah last. If she's not there, I don't know what I'll do next.

I've been there a million times, but I never pay much attention to where I'm going. I'm always too busy picking up interesting messages on fire hydrants and trees along the way. Then I catch up to the kids when Brian calls me.

I'm in the middle of the town now. It's getting dark. There are pretty lights strung up across the street and a big tree with lights in the town square. There is music playing, too.

Here's that big store that Brian likes. I know because I've waited outside this store when Brian and Josh went inside to look at toys and stuff. There are toys in the window, and there's the thing that Brian wants for Christmas. He showed it to Josh last time we were here. It's a big box with lots of little jars in it. I think it's called a mystery set.

But this isn't getting me any closer to Tallulah. I know that Dougie's farm is just outside of the town, where the houses get far apart. I pick a direction and start walking. My breath makes little clouds. I'm not watching where I'm going, so I bump into some people with packages. One man drops a big box and yells at me. Then I run through a bunch of people singing Christmas songs in front of a house. Fa-la-la-la-la? What kind of peoplespeak is that?

I keep running along the road until there are no more houses. I'm coming to a curve. Is there a curve before Dougie's? I can't remember. I'm looking for that Christmas tree on Dougie's silo, but I don't see it. I don't smell chicken manure, either. Maybe I came the wrong way.

Suddenly there's a bright light in my eyes. Then the blast of a horn. I try to run, but it's coming too fast. It's a huge truck. It doesn't hit me, but the wind it makes blows me into a big snowdrift. It takes me a few minutes to catch my breath and dig out of the snow. I don't like it here. I start running back into town, looking over my shoulder every few steps to make sure there isn't another truck coming behind me.

When I get back into the middle of the town, I head out the other side. Good thing this is a small town. A dog could wear himself out doing this. I can still hear those people singing in the distance. I like Christmas. Last year I got a new soft doggie bed and a purple ball with a squeaker in it. I love that bed. I still have the ball, too, but the squeaker doesn't work anymore. I wonder if Brian got me a new toy this year?

It's really dark now and I'm getting scared. But wait! There's the silo with the Christmas tree on top. And I sniff the heavenly smell of chicken manure. Yep, that's Dougie's place. I go right up to the barn, climb on an old wagon, and look into the window. I can see hens dozing by the flickering light of the TV. I think I've spotted Tallulah, but it's too dark to tell for sure.

I don't want to wake up the other hens. I can still feel all the places they pecked me the other day, and I'm not going through *that* again. I poke my nose through the crack in the door and nudge it open. The smell of chicken manure hits me right in the face. Wooo Hoo! Chickens really smell great! I twitch my nose, trying to sort out Tallulah's scent from the rest. I got it! She's here!

I tiptoe slowly into the barn, following Tallulah's scent. There she is, shivering on a low roost away from all the others. She's still wearing the sweater, but it's all dirty now. I guess that's why chickens don't usually wear clothes. It's hard to keep clean when you live in a barn.

"Psst!" I say.

She opens one eye. Then both—wide. "Arful!"

"Shhh! Don't wake everybody up. I came to take you home."

Tallulah sticks her beak in the air. "Maybe I don't want to go. Maybe I like it here. Maybe somebody here likes *me*—a lot!"

All of a sudden I see something big coming at me. It's Herman! I start running, but he flattens me just before I reach the door. I close my eyes, waiting for the next blow, but nothing happens.

"Take her."

I open my eyes. "What?"

Herman is smiling across the barn at Tallulah. He's trying to whisper to me without moving his beak. "Take her. She's a pain in the gizzard."

I try to swallow, which isn't easy when you have a twenty-five-pound rooster standing on your chest.

"You . . . want me to take Tallulah?" I have to make sure I'm hearing this right. Herman has a really thick rooster accent.

"Yes! And don't ever let her come back. She's driving me nuts with the math problems."

"Hi, sweetie!" Tallulah calls out. "Don't hurt Arful. He was just leaving."

"I'll pretend I'm not watching," Herman whispers. "Try to make it look like a kidnapping." He jumps off me and struts across the barn, his glossy tail waving like a flag. Then he settles in on a roost, winks, and pretends to fall asleep.

I sneak over to Tallulah, jump up on my hind legs, and try to grab her in my mouth, but all I get is sweater. I clamp my teeth down on it and run, dragging her along with me. Just as I get through the door, I hear Herman crow, "Come back here with my girl-friend!" Nice touch, Herman.

I push the door closed behind me.

Tallulah smiles. "Isn't that sweet? He adores me, but of course, who wouldn't?"

I feel a thud against the door as Herman hits it with his full weight. "I'll get you for this, you . . . you very sneaky dog." Herman is a lousy actor.

"So that's why you wanted to stay?" I ask Tallulah. "You're in love with Herman the Terminator?"

Tallulah straightens out her sweater. "Don't be silly. Herman might be handsome, but he's much too bossy. Besides, we have absolutely nothing in common. He's terrible at math. He does worship the ground I walk on, though. Poor thing." She jumps up on my back. "Giddyap, garbage breath! I want to go home now."

"Hey! You can walk on your own two feet."

"*Au contraire,* skuzzy hair. My poor little tootsies would freeze in all this snow. Brian will be very upset

if you let that happen. I'm sure he's already mad at you for not being a good bodyguard."

"I was just supposed to protect you from getting hurt. Nobody said I had to keep you from running away."

"Brian doesn't know I ran away. He probably thinks you let me go on purpose, which, of course, you did. I'll bet he never wants to see you again."

I don't answer her, but I know she's right. I'm not even sure Brian will forgive me if I bring her home. I start walking. Tallulah's sharp toenails are digging into my back, but I keep on walking.

All of a sudden I feel pecking on my head. "Hey, what are you doing?"

"Snacking on fleas. I'm hungry."

I think about the fact that I could just eat her right here on the side of the road and nobody would ever know. The thought of fresh chicken makes me drool. Before long I have a little fringe of icicles hanging off my lips.

I have a long argument with myself as I walk along. I finally decide not to eat Tallulah, because the only thing that will save Brian is to have her come home alive.

And besides, when your meal is eating the fleas off your head, it kind of kills your appetite.

Chapter Nine

It's a long walk, but when we get back into town, I don't have any trouble finding our house. We go through my doggie door. Mrs. Lewis has finished decorating the Christmas tree with strings of popcorn and cranberries and her cookies. There's a big pile of wrapped packages under the tree, but nobody is around. They've all gone to bed.

"Good thing Brian isn't up," Tallulah says. "He'd probably throw you right back out in the cold."

I nose around at the gifts. There's no big fluffy dog bed this year. Probably no dog bones, either. At least I don't smell any.

"You think there's a present for you under that tree?" Tallulah cackles. "Fat chance, mange belly!"

I poke at a few of the soft packages to see if they have squeaky toys inside. Nope. Not a sound. I have a lump in my throat. Tallulah is right. There's no present for me this year.

"Hey, drool bucket, I'm hungry," Tallulah says. "What's for dinner?"

"I don't know. There might be something in my dog dish." I sniff the air. "Nope. Don't smell a thing." That clinches it. Brian didn't even expect me to come back. Probably didn't want me to come back.

Tallulah is picking her way through the packages. "Oh, puh-leeeze! Do I look like the kind of chicken who would stoop to eat dog food?" She looks up at the tree. "Hey, what're those funny-looking things on the tree? Cookies?"

"Sort of," I say.

"What do you mean, sort of? Are they cookies or not?"

"Yeah, they're cookies, but I don't think you want to eat them."

She gives me a sly smile—at least as much of a smile as a chicken beak can manage. "Trying to trick me, huh? You don't want me to eat any of the cookies because you want them all to yourself?"

"Believe me, I'm not even tempted."

"Yeah, right!" She knocks a cookie to the floor and

begins pecking at it. Then her eyes scrunch up and she spits it out. "Phfttt! Patooey! Blechhhh! You're trying to poison me. These aren't cookies!"

"They're Mrs. Lewis's cookies. They're good for you."

Tallulah struts around under the tree, looking up at the decorations. "What's that puffy yellow stuff?"

"Popcorn. Mrs. Lewis pops it and puts it on a string."

"Corn? I like corn." She pulls at a string until it breaks. Popcorn falls all over the floor and she scarfs one up. "Now, this is more like it."

"Cut that out," I say. "That's just to make the tree look pretty. You're not supposed to eat it. I ate some when I was a puppy and got in a lot of trouble. Of course I ate the string, too. That was a big mistake."

She plucks at another string. Cranberries are bouncing all over the rug now. "Mmm. I have two of the major food groups here. If this tree has bugs on it, I'll have a complete balanced meal."

She tugs at the popcorn again. A glass ornament shakes loose and heads for the floor. I catch it in my mouth without breaking it and place it carefully on the couch cushion. Now she's pulling at the cranberries again. "Knock it off," I say.

"I did knock it off and you caught it. Heads up, slobber chops. Here comes another one."

There isn't time to argue with her. I'm too busy rescuing falling ornaments. By the time she has eaten her fill, I have three glass balls, two pimiento Santa cookies, and a little herbal wreath on the couch. There are cranberries, popcorn, and bare strings all over the floor. I run around, slurping up the leftovers, being careful not to eat the string. I'm not going through *that* again.

I know I'll probably get in trouble for this even though Tallulah made the mess. I'll be lucky if Brian doesn't kick me out of the house when he comes downstairs in the morning. The more I think of it, the more worried I get. Maybe I should just get this over with. I'll wake up Brian and tell him Tallulah is back. If he forgives me, then everything is fine. If not . . . well, I'll think about that later. I head for the stairs.

"I wouldn't go up there," Tallulah says. "If you keep quiet, you can spend one more night in a warm house."

She may be right, but I have to take a chance. I run up the stairs and push against Brian's door, but it doesn't budge. I even try scratching on the door, but he doesn't wake up. I don't want to bark and wake everybody, so I go back downstairs. I squeeze behind the couch.

Tallulah is watching. "Doesn't want to see you, does he, kibble breath?"

"None of your business."

"Whatever. I'm not the one in trouble here." She flies up to the top branch and settles in. "Nighty-night."

I think I'm too worried to sleep, but I must drift off. Next thing I know it's daylight and I can hear the whole family coming down the stairs. Tallulah is sleeping on the top of the tree. She looks like the world's ugliest tree angel. They pass right by the living room and go into the kitchen to have breakfast. I can't hear what they're saying. Pretty soon I hear the clanking of dishes in the sink, and they all come into the living room.

Mrs. Lewis looks at the tree. "My goodness. I thought I had more cranberry and popcorn garlands on the tree."

Dr. Lewis starts to sit down on the couch, then stops himself. "Whoa! I almost sat on these ornaments. You must have been interrupted in the middle of your decorating, dear."

Mrs. Lewis shakes her head. "Well, I guess that would explain the garlands. There's just so much to do before Christmas, I get distracted. I can't believe Christmas is coming tomorrow. I haven't even made all of my cookies yet."

"Oh, I think we have more than enough cookies, dear." Dr. Lewis settles on the couch and pats the space beside him. "Just relax and enjoy the holidays. Brian, have you tried to guess what your presents are?"

"Not yet, Dad." Brian sits down in front of the packages without noticing Tallulah asleep in the tree. He has his back to me.

"What about that big one in the red wrapping?" Mrs. Lewis says.

Brian picks up the red box and gives it a little shake. This is my favorite part of Christmas. I love to sit next to Brian when he's trying to figure out what's in the packages. He usually asks me what I think is inside.

I'm a great guesser, but in all those other years, I couldn't tell Brian what I knew. Now I can talk! I want to tell him that this red one smells just like that store he and the other guys love. This present has to be that mystery set he wants. I can even hear the little jars clinking together and something sloshing around inside them.

I'm all ready to slip in beside him and whisper in his ear, when he puts down the package and turns around a little so I can see his face. He looks awful. He's still mad!

"Aren't you going to make a guess, Brian?" Mrs. Lewis asks.

Brian shrugs. "Maybe later."

"Look, son," Dr. Lewis says, "I know you're upset about Arful and that chicken, but you can't let that ruin your whole Christmas."

This is breaking my heart. Brian loves Christmas. It's his favorite day of the whole year. And now he's going to get the present he's always wanted, but he won't care about it because I lost Tallulah. I don't want to come out of hiding, but I have to make Brian look up and see Tallulah sleeping on top of the tree. Then everything will be all right.

I notice a cranberry on the rug near my nose. I pick it up and hold it gently between my lips, then aim and blow it hard. This is a game I play a lot with acorns when I want to annoy squirrels, so I'm pretty good at it. Sure enough, I hit Tallulah right in the head. She wakes up with a squawk and tumbles right out of the tree, knocking off a couple more of those glass balls on the way down.

Mrs. Lewis screams, which sets Tallulah flapping all over the room.

"Tallulah!" Brian yells. "I thought I'd never see you again."

He has this big smile on his face now. He's happy because he has his chicken back.

Dr. Lewis jumps up and grabs Tallulah as she tries to fly over his head. "What's this thing she's wearing?"

"It's a sweater," Mrs. Lewis says. "I thought . . . well, it's a long story."

Brian peeks over his mother's shoulder. "Is she all right?"

"I think she'll be fine, dear. I'm going to make her a mega-vitamin meal to build her strength just in case. I just got some fresh seaweed from the health food store today."

Tallulah blinks. "Seaweed! What do I look like, a fish?"

Mrs. Lewis smiles. "There, she must be feeling better. She's clucking. Isn't that sweet?"

"Sweet!" Tallulah squawks. "*Sweet!* Read my beak! I don't eat slimy green stuff!"

Dr. and Mrs. Lewis take Tallulah into the kitchen, but Brian walks over to the living room window and just stands there, staring outside. Could he be looking for me? "Hey, Brian," I whisper, but he doesn't answer. Maybe he heard me and just doesn't *want* to answer. I slip out from under the couch and get right behind him.

I probably shouldn't do it, but I can't help myself. I lick his fingers.

Chapter Ten

"Arful?" All of a sudden Brian is on his knees, giving me the world's biggest hug. He's crying! "Arful, I thought you were mad at me for yelling at you. I thought you ran away forever."

"I thought you were mad at me for losing Tallulah," I say, licking his face. His tears taste salty. "I helped Tallulah get away, but I didn't mean for her to get lost. She tricked me. She said she was going into Dougie's house to get me a cookie, but she ran off instead."

"I shouldn't have blamed you," Brian says, wiping his eyes. "I'm so glad you're back."

I hear the *skritch* of chicken feet as Tallulah comes back into the room. Her beak is green. "Yuck, yuck, pah-tooey! Seaweed will never cross these chicken lips again!" She looks at me. "You're supposed to protect me, slime mouth."

"Oh, I can't protect you from Mrs. Lewis. She's the boss around here. She makes me eat seaweed all the time. Tofu and wheat germ, too. Awful stuff." Brian looks up, but I'm talking in dogspeak, so he doesn't understand.

Tallulah fluffs out her feathers. "Well, if she tries anything else, I'll poke her eyes out. I don't like that stupid kid, either."

"Stupid kid? Do you know how worried Brian was about you? I'm not going to let you hurt his feelings. You be nice to him."

"Me? *Nice?* Fat chance, meathead. I don't have to be nice to anybody."

Mrs. Lewis comes into the room. Her hair is all messed up and she has green stains on her blouse. When she sees me, she rushes over and gives me a kiss on the top of my head. "Arful! Oh, I'm so glad you came back! We were terribly worried about you."

Tallulah walks by and gives Mrs. Lewis a dirty look.

"Our little chicken is quite a handful," Mrs. Lewis says. "I've always been very fond of animals, but this one is . . . well, difficult. She certainly doesn't like seaweed."

"No kidding!" Tallulah clucks. She pecks at my tail. "Hey, flea farm! I need some nice, juicy bugs to get the yucky taste out of my mouth. Go find some for me. Something bigger than fleas."

"Where am I going to find bugs in the middle of the winter?"

"You figure it out, dribble lips. I give the orders, you obey them. You're just my bodyguard."

That's it. I've had enough of her. "You know what? You can find your own bugs and guard your own body. I quit!"

I go back and sit under the tree with Brian. I rest my chin on his knee so I get a good sniff at each present as he picks it up and shakes it. Tallulah hangs around us, making rotten remarks. Once Brian asks me what she's squawking about.

"Oh, nothing," I say.

"I didn't realize a chicken could be such a trouble-maker. Is she saying nasty things to you? Because if she is, I'll make her stop."

"I'm not paying any attention to her," I say, which makes Tallulah really mad. She stomps around the room with jerky steps, like a robot with rusty joints.

Later that afternoon the doorbell rings. Doorbells always make me bark. I don't know why, but I just can't help myself. It's "ding-dong, barkity-bark" every time. I rush to the door thinking it's Josh and Dougie, but one sniff tells me that Emily is the one standing on the front steps.

Suddenly I have an idea. While Mrs. Lewis goes to answer the door, I run over and whisper to Brian. He nods.

Emily comes in with a smug little smile on her face, but her eyes get wide when she sees Tallulah. "She's still here?"

"Of course," Brian says. "Where else would she be? I told you, she's been just fine the whole time."

Emily gets that squinty look that means she thinks Brian is lying, which, of course, he is.

"Let me take your coat, Emily," Mrs. Lewis says. "I have fresh soybean Christmas cookies with spinach sprinkles. Would you like some?" Everybody in town knows about Mrs. Lewis's cookies, and nobody wants any. Even starving stray dogs won't eat them.

"Oh, no thanks, Mrs. Lewis," Emily says, backing away. "I just stopped in to deliver Tallulah's Christmas present." She reaches into the little silver bag and pulls out something pink and puffy.

"What's that thing?" Brian asks.

Emily rolls her eyes. "It's a ballet tutu. Isn't that just the cutest little outfit?"

"Oh, how sweet," Mrs. Lewis says. "Let's see how she looks in it."

"They're not making me wear that thing," Tallulah says. But Emily and Mrs. Lewis gang up on Tallulah and get her into the dress before she has a chance to escape. There's even a little sparkly thing that fastens to her head with elastic.

"A tiny tiara, too?" Mrs. Lewis claps her hands. "Did you ever see anything so sweet? And look! She's dancing."

Tallulah is running around the room in circles. "Get me out of this ugly thing!"

"You never looked better," I say. "Pink is definitely your color."

All of a sudden Brian grabs Tallulah and shoves her into Emily's arms. "I want you to take Tallulah home as my Christmas present to you, Emily."

Emily gasps. "Really? Are you sure?"

"Well, you're so good at making clothes for her and all. She'll be much happier with you." Brian turns to me and winks.

"That's very generous of you, dear," Mrs. Lewis says. "I know how much that chicken means to you. Just let me get a clean sweater for Tallulah, Emily.

And I'll pack up some seaweed. She's not fond of it, but you really should make sure she eats it."

"Oh, this will be so much fun," Emily says. "I'm going to dress her up in all my doll clothes. She can play with my parrot."

Tallulah's head is bobbing around like one of those toy dogs some people have in their cars. "Forget the seaweed, and I'm not playing with a parrot. It's just talk talk talk with those birds. They can drive you nuts. I'm staying here."

"No, you're not," I say. "You're going to Emily's."

"If I do, I'll make that girl's life miserable."

"Fine with me. You and Emily deserve each other." I can feel my tail wagging.

"I can't wait to get her home," Emily says. "I'm going to have Cara and Lissa come over with their doll clothes. We can dress her up all day today and every day of vacation next week."

"If you have one of those doll baby bottles, you could feed Tallulah some seaweed juice," Mrs. Lewis says. "You might want to wrap her up tight in a baby blanket while you do it to keep her from being too . . . uh . . . active."

"Oooooh, that will be so much fun!" Emily squeals. "Just like taking care of a real baby!"

"Arful! Help me!" Tallulah shrieks as Emily carries her out the door.

"Sorry, that's not my job anymore," I say. And I push the door closed with my nose.

Chapter Eleven

It's Christmas morning. Brian opens a package that has a baseball glove inside and puts the wrapping over my head. I run around with it, loving the wonderful smell of leather on the crackly paper. Then I go back and snuggle up to Brian. My tail is whacking against the floor so hard, it's making the Christmas lights quiver.

"Open this one now, Brian." Mrs. Lewis hands him the red box.

He gives it a shake. "Do you know what this is, Arful?"

I say yes in dogspeak, but it just sounds like "woof." Brian knows what I mean.

Mrs. Lewis laughs. "Isn't that cute? It sounded like Arful was answering Brian's question."

"Is it something I'll like?" Brian asks.

"You bet!" I woof, and everybody laughs.

Brian rips the red paper off the package. "Wow! My chemistry set! You got me the super deluxe one with the extra experiments."

"You even get a Bunsen burner with this," Dr. Lewis says. "It's supposed to be for older kids, but you're so good at reading and following directions, I think you can handle it. We can try some experiments together to get you started."

"Wow, that's great! Thanks, Dad!"

Brian opens the box and reads the labels on the jars, then looks up. "Hey, Arful, I almost forgot. Come here."

I run over and lick his face.

Brian is looking for something under the tree. "There's another gift in here somewhere. Wait. I found it. This one's for you." He holds out a small package wrapped in shiny green paper. "Merry Christmas, Arful."

Do I hear something when I take it in my mouth? I'm not sure. I try not to sniff, because I want to be surprised. I hold it gently with my paw while I rip off the paper.

"Maybe you won't like it," Brian says. "After what happened and all."

I pull the last of the paper away. It's a new squeaky toy in the shape of a chicken. The squeaker even sounds like a chicken, but I wonder if the people who made the toy know what it says? Every time I bite down, the chicken's little rubber wings flap up and it cries, "Help me!" in chickenspeak.

"I don't like my present," I whisper to Brian. "I *love* it!" I squeak it about ten times in a row. This is the best Christmas present I ever got in my whole life!

I run around the house, biting the chicken. "Help me! Help me! Help me! Help me! Help me! Help me!"

My whole family is watching me and laughing. Hoooo-boy! Life doesn't get any better than this!